Short Story Collection

Books by Ron Mueller

The Alex Evercrest Series-Detective
    The River Front
    The Girl on the Grill
    Missing
    Maggot
    Racist
    Votive Candles
    Windy City
    Country Road
    Pool of Blood
    Sins of the Daughter

The Door Series-Science Fiction
    The Door

The Savitar Series-Science Fiction
    Journey's End
    Savitar
    Confluence

Bram Nielson Series-Science Fiction
    The Fold
    The Message
    Fold Wormhole
    Negative Fold
    Ripples in Time

The Taelo Series-Prehistory America
    Taelo: The Early Years
    Taelo: The Golden Feather
    Taelo: Journey of Discovery
    Taelo: Dangerous Passage
    Taelo: Condor Clan Slingers
    Taelo: Circumvention
    Taelo: The Journey of Sages
    Taelo: Collection

A Taelo Story
    The Name of the Child
    White Swan and Quiet Pheasant
    Broken Spear
    Floating Cloud
    Quiet Rabbit
    Busy Bee
    Little Otter& Talking Wren
    Burley Bear & Meadow Flower

A Feather-in-the-Wind Story
    The Eastern Elk Clan

The Problem Solver Series-Secret Agent
    The Beginning
    Drug Lords
    Border Crosser

Current Past and Future-Science Fiction
Event Survivors-Science Fiction
The Door-Science Fiction
Viajante 7-Science Fiction
Imagination by Courtney Huynh and Chloe Parker

Short Stories Collection
By: *Ron Mueller*

Around the World Publishing LLC
4914 Cooper Road Suite 144
Cincinnati, Ohio 45242-9998

Short Stories Collection, by Ron Mueller Copyright © 2023

ISBN 13: 978-1-68223-404-4
ISBN 10: 1-68223-404-5

Distributed by Ingram
Cincinnati Scene by: Nagel Photography @ Shutterstock
Smiling Face by: Sweepea @Morguefiles
Indian Maiden by: Jozef Klopacka @ Shutterstock
Cover Picture by: Hongqi Zhang @ Dreamstime
Ocean Scene by: Hien Mueller
Cover Design by: Ron Mueller

Ron Mueller

Table of Content

Ron Mueller

The Boy With the Radiant Smile

His smile was contagious. It lit up the room. She could not forget it. Every time she remembered it she felt better. It was one of the few things she could remember. The problem was she couldn't remember who she was and didn't know anything about the boy with the smile.

Angela looked up the steep bank. The rain was heavy, and the water was running swiftly past her body. She was in danger of being swept farther down the hill. There was a side trench where only a small stream of water was gushing down. She could not stand. Her ankle was twisted, and the pain almost made her pass out. She crawled up into the trench. The water ran under her and joined the larger stream. Her feet were the only part of her body still in the larger torrent.

Sometime later the sun shining on her face woke her from her dream. She had been dreaming about the boy with the smile. She was sorry to wake up.

"Who am I," flashed through her mind.

She was dry on her top side but still wet on her backside. Her ankle was swollen and hurt. She had a huge bump on her head.

As she looked around she realized she was alone and had no clue where she was. She decided to crawl up the trench she was in. It got smaller as she went up. She was able to push with her with her good left foot and pull with her arms. It took her a good hour to crawl up the trench to where it came out on a black top road. Across the road was a huge boulder. She crawled to it and got into the shade. She put her back to the boulder and rested.

"My name is …," but nothing came to her.

How had she gotten to this location?

She was dressed in canvass slacks, had on hiking boots and a short sleeve blouse. She wondered what she looked like.

She checked her pockets. They were empty.

She was dressed as if she were going hiking. Surely she had to have something with her. She decided to look down to where she had awakened.

There was nothing there. She scanned along the trail where she remembered the water had run like a small stream. Down almost to at the bottom, caught on a limb was what appeared to be a backpack. The branch holding it had kept it from being swept into the small creek below.

She wished she could remember her name.

The only thing she remembered was the picture of the boy with the contagious smile. It made her feel good.

She went back into the shade of the boulder. She knew the boulder was important, but she had no clue why. The road was a narrow single lane road. Either it was a long driveway or a very little used road. She was not sure if the leaves and twigs had been washed onto it by the rain during the night or if it was just not used.

She was almost dry. She decided to test her foot. She used the boulder to prop herself up. She could tell her foot was tight in her boot. She did not want to loosen it until she could test it with her weight.

"Ouch. I am going to have to wait some more before I try to walk on this foot," she thought to herself. She sat back down in the shade.

The grumble from her stomach reminded her of the backpack.

"I'll bet there is something to eat in it," she thought and with that she made up her mind.

She tried hopping on one foot but that hurt almost as much a trying to step on her bad foot. She decided to crawl on her hands and knees until she was just above the spot where her backpack was snagged. She found a promising spot to make her way down.

She was a little panicked by not knowing who she was. She decided to focus on her backpack and breakfast.

"Who was the good-looking guy and the devastating smile," she thought as she worked her way down to the backpack.

"And how am I going to get back up," flashed through her mind as she looked back up the bank.

The backpack did indeed have food in it. It was muddy on the outside, but the contents were packed in baggies, were dry, and fresh. It had snagged on a low hanging branch of a bush and had been in the shade. There was an extra t shirt, underwear, food, comb, and a notebook with writing. There was also a name on the backpack, Angela.

"I must be Angela, or I was using Angela's backpack," she thought to herself. She waited patiently to see if any other visions or memory would come to her. She felt the huge bump on the side of her head.

After a few bites from one of the sandwiches, she decided to drag the backpack and scoot the rest of the way down the trail to the small stream about thirty feet away. On the way down she spotted a bed roll washed up under another bush.

"Well, I must have come out here to camp. I guess I am a wood's girl," she thought to herself.

There was a high little peninsula where the stream made an s turn. Angela could tell it was a high spot by the grasses and small limbs that had washed and been dropped around it when the stream rose. There was a perfect sitting stone on the downstream side.

She threw her backpack in the shade of a small bush. She unrolled the bed roll and found it was made up of a sleeping bag and a single person tent. She unrolled them so they would dry out. Then she decided to wash up and soak her foot in the cool water.

She took off her left boot, rolled up her slacks and after taking off her socks put that foot in the water.

She turned her attention to taking of the boot from her hurt ankle. She loosened the laces until the boot was totally open. The only thing keeping it on was the size of her foot and ankle. She slowly worked her foot out of the boot. Sweat was rolling down into her eyes as she grimaced and slowly worked her foot out of the boot. She was almost crying by the time her foot cleared the boot. It looked gross. It was at least twice the size of her left ankle and foot. She slowly put it into the cool water of the stream.

She leaned back on the grassy bank and fell asleep.

Some minnows nibbling at her toes woke her up. The sun was getting low in the sky, so Angela knew it was late afternoon. She looked back up toward the road. She was not going to climb up there tonight. Her ankle felt better. It was still hurting but the swelling had gone down. The right foot was only twice the size of the left foot. The lump on her head was down in size too, only about as big as a plum.

She crawled up to the top of camp area and lay across her sleeping bag. The sun had done its job and the bag was dry. She wished she could build a fire but gathering the wood was out of the question. She checked her backpack and sure enough she had come prepared with matches in a waterproof container. If she remained here more than another day she would figure out how to get some wood and make a fire.

She was Angela but she still did not know who she was. She knew by the preparation and the things in her backpack, Angela was an outdoors girl. When she went through the notebook it became clear she had some talent in drawing and in writing.

There was a very good pencil sketch of a chipmunk and a little story about it. The only other consistent thing she could remember was the boy with the radiant smile. Who was he and what was he to her? Why was he the only thing coming back to her?

Angela knew exactly how to set up her single person tent and sleeping bag. She had no recollection how she knew this, but she could tell she had done this many times before. Even on her hands and knees she got the job done quickly.

The sunset burned an orange strip along the distant mountains and highlighted the grey clouds still in the sky. Angela sat with her feet in the water, eating her second sandwich. She was still confused but she was relaxed. She was coming to the realization she was capable and in her element. She might not remember her name, but she was confident in herself.

The multitude of stars against the pure black of space verified the weather was clearing. Angela lay warmly in her sleeping bag enjoying studying the various constellations. She could see the sweep of the stars of the Milky Way. The evening air felt good against the bump on her head. The cold water in the stream had made her ankle feel better. She hoped by morning she could put her boot back on and walk. She fell asleep thinking about the boy with the radiant smile.

An owl hooted somewhere nearby. The gurgling of the stream provided a soft awakening call. Angela slowly came awake and wondered where she was. She could feel the cool morning air on her face. The sun was not yet up but was threatening the edged of the world out on the other side of the valley.

The last she remembered was packing and planning to go on a hike for the weekend.

Her friend Marian had backed out at the last minute and Angela decided to go on her own. She had planned out this adventure for weeks. It was the first event of the summer vacation. She had hiked up the mountain and was following a stream down the other side when the rain had blown in. According to the weatherman it was supposed to remain clear all weekend.

"So much for believing the weatherman," Angela thought when the rain began.

Angela was slowly remembering the events previous to having slipped and hit her head. It was a mystery how she had ended up at this camp. She sat up and looked around. She recognized the surrounding landscape. She was in Huntsman Valley. This was a valley high in the mountains. She must be camped next to Swallow Creek. This valley was supposed to be the home of the ghost of an ancient Indian Princess. This Princess was said to wander the valley protecting the animals from harm.

Angela had wanted to come up to the valley to draw the various small animals and to write a story about the Princess.

She sat up and rummaged through her backpack. She had packed some fishing line and two lures. She decided to try her hand at catching a trout or two for breakfast. There was a small frying pan packed in the backpack. She took out her small hunting knife and put it in her cargo pocket. She had come prepared.

She tried standing on her foot and decided crawling would work better. She washed her face and put her feet in the water. The water was cold enough to hurt as she put her right foot into the water. Soon it was numb and actually felt good.

There were several clumps of small wood caught in the brush along the stream. She could see enough within crawling distance to make a small fire. She crawled around gathering the wood. She wished Marian had come with her.

A rabbit hopping along on the other side of the creek caused her to stop and pick up her pad and pencil. She did a quick sketch of the rabbit. It was a perfect subject. It seemed to know it was being drawn sat still watching her. As she finished the rabbit disappeared into the high grass.

She was finally ready to try her hand at fishing. She estimated the time to be about eight in the morning. The air was still moist with the morning dew and the rays of the sun painted the few morning clouds in the sky a light yellow.

She could not remember setting up her camp. The last she remembered was starting down into the valley as the thunder boomed and the sky open up and dropped what seemed to be buckets of water down on her head. She knew no one expected her back for several days. She could probably be gone for a week before anyone would raise the alarm.

She could not remember anyone in her family. She felt disoriented. She remembered Marian but no one else.

She looked back at her small camp and froze. Sitting cross legged next to the unlit campfire was a ghost.

Angela could see through it but at the same time she could see the long hair fall across one shoulder. The intricate bead design of the vest and the fringes of the dress indicated they were leather.

The posture and position of her ghost conveyed a sense of power and grandeur.

It was the Indian Princess.

Angela flipped her pad to a new page and sketched the scene. She was mesmerized.

The Princess gestured indicating she should come closer. Angela obeyed and crawled closer. She was now sitting cross legged across the campfire from the ghost.

The princess had a sad beauty. She was the same size as Angela. She pointed to a spot in the ground by the pile of wood making up the campfire. Angela had carefully cleared the area to ensure containment of the fire.

There in the soil she saw an object.

She leaned forward and with a small stick excavated around the object.

She uncovered a gold chain.

She continued to carefully dig it out and found it attached to a bone carving.

It was a replica of the Princess as she was now sitting. Angela drew furiously as she captured the moment on several pages of her journal.

She knew people would think her crazy, but she would have the evidence of this meeting both in the drawings and in the gold chain with the bone carving of the Princess.

The Princess slowly disappeared.

Later, she was successful at catching two trout. They made an excellent breakfast. She was set for the day and knew she would be able to survive until her ankle let her walk out of the valley.

The stream was only about six feet wide and about two feet at the deepest. Angela took off all her clothes and went skinny dipping. It felt great to clean up. She rinsed the mud out of the blouse she had been wearing and took out the spare she had found in her backpack. She lay on her tent to dry off.

The sun was now high in the sky and the air had turned warm. She decided trout for a late lunch or early dinner would do fine.

She hoped the Princes would pay her another visit.

A hawk high in the sky caught her attention next and once again the drawing pad came out.

She spent the entire day within crawling distance of the camp.

Once again the Sun lit the horizon and turned the sky a deep red and then it faded slowly into the black of night. The multitude of stars once again ushered in sleep.

Angela awoke the next morning to the memory of the boy with the beautiful smile. She knew he was close to her. She felt the connection.

She stood up and tested her ankle. This would be the day she would continue her journey. She was going to back track to the point she first remembered. She put on her boots and laced them up snuggly. Her sprained ankle was still swollen but was almost back to its original size. It was already turning a sickly purple and yellow. It hurt but she would be able to walk on it.

She cleaned the camp and put the grass she had removed back where the fire had been. When she was done it was hard to tell she had camped at this spot for almost two days. She hoped the Princess approved.

She felt the locket she was wearing around her neck. She knew she had slept on the same ground as the Princess. The locket around her neck was proof the Princess had been real. She looked out over the valley and took in the scene.

She flipped through her notebook to see if she had captured the key points in her sketches. She turned to go back up the trail when out across the valley she saw something sparkle. The sun was hitting some object. Attracted by the shiny sparkle, she decided on a new direction.

She knew distances were always farther than they appeared. She hoped she could make it across the valley during the day. It was early summer and there would be few berries. She kept her eye out for dew berries and early wild onions. The second was more for flavoring if she found anything to cook. She hoped the object she was tracking was close to the stream.

She locked in the location of the sparkle. It was located directly below the large crack in the cliff facing her. The split seemed to point at whatever was making the light sparkle.

She crossed the meandering stream several times. When she was close to the cliff and came upon the stream for the third time she decided it was time to set up camp. Her foot felt fine, but her stomach was complaining.

For the third time that day she had fish. She had no complaints about the situation. She was very happy to catch a large trout on her first throw. She actually had to fight to drag it up on the rocky bank of the stream.

It was a beauty.

This time an Owl landed not too far from where she had thrown the cleanings from the fish. He was out looking for his evening meal. He seemed to sit and study Angela as she rendered a sketch of him.

She was in a quiet conversation with him when she saw the fox make off with the pieces of fish and skin she had tossed behind the rocks.

She chuckled as she thought of the childhood story of the Owl and the Fox her father had told her.

Her father, she tried to see her father but failed. Her memory seemed to be slowly coming back.

The setting sun caused the object up by the cliff to give off one more wink. It seemed to be making sure she knew where to look.

It was hard for her to go to sleep but finally sleep overtook her. Once again she dreamed of the boy with the radiant smile.

The next morning the hike up to the spot at the base of the cliff took almost to noon. Once she arrived at the approximate location of where she thought the object attracting her was located, Angela decided she needed to set up a search pattern.

The object had to be out in the open. There were not too many locations where an object could be and be seen across the valley. She took out her sketch pad and drew a perspective of the area.

Then she began to look at all the points high enough to be seen across the valley.

She had given up when not more than twenty feet from where she had dejectedly sat down she saw the sparkle.

With a whoop, she jumped up and almost fell down when she planted her right foot. The pain was still there. She hobbled over to find out what she had been hunting.

She was stunned to find a silver pendant on a silver chain.

She flipped to her drawings and there in her drawing of the Princess was the pendant. It was hanging around the Princess's neck.

There was no question it was the same one. Every detail was the same.

It was magical.

There was nothing else around. A search of the area turned up nothing else.

Angela made her way back to previous evening's camp. She would spend the night and then hike back out of the valley the way she had come in.

She had not caught a fish in the evening and gone to sleep hungry. Her luck was better in the morning, and she felt satisfied as she began her hike back across the valley. Her ankle was feeling much better, and she was hiking faster than when she had come across.

She made it to the trail on the other side by early afternoon.

She was deciding on whether to try to get out of the valley at this moment or to wait until the next morning. There seemed to be something unfinished about her visit to the valley.

She felt uneasy and she was still very disoriented about not remembering who she was. She looked over toward where her original camp had been two evenings ago.

There just past the camp on the next knoll sat the Princess. This time Angela walked without any hesitation toward her. The shimmering presence seemed to have a smile on her lips. She gestured to herself and then gestured to the mound they were sitting on.

Angela knew immediately she was sitting on the Princes' grave. She went over to the edge of the stream and collected a set of rocks. She put up a marker so she could in the future return to this very spot.

She decided that she would build a monument to the Princess of the valley.

That evening she went to sleep once more wondering about the boy with the radiant smile.

Morning found Angela ready to head home. Home she thought. She hoped she would remember where home was and who lived there.

She still could not remember who she was. All she knew was she would head up the trail she had come down. She would go to where it met the small road and then she would see where it would lead.

Her hike took her parallel to the small road. The trail seemed to keep just below the road. She had a sense it would parallel the road most of the way.

Her morning breakfast had worn off and she was feeling hungry as she continued to hike along. The sun reached its zenith when ahead and up the valley she spotted what appeared to be a small town.

That's my hometown flashed through her mind, but the thought did not fully open the pathways. Her past was still lost in the murky grey of her mind. She was now getting impatient with her condition.

"Maybe I should hit myself with a rock on the other side of my head," she said out loud.

She continued at a faster pace. She hoped she would know where her home was located. She at least figured someone would know her and give her directions to her house. Her ankle was now tired, and she was beginning to limp. She would love to have a long hot bath when she got home.

Then she heard the singing coming from somewhere ahead. It was up on the road. The voice and the song instantly triggered her. She scrambled up the slope to the road.

"Wow, right on time," the boy with the radiant smile said from the two seated bicycle. "I can't believe you timed it so perfectly.

Angela had a huge smile on her face. She knew it was just as radiant as the one on the boy in front of her. She remembered everything and she was happy.

The boy with the radiant smile was her twin brother.

The End

Three Dimensional Love

ℱor the last few years, Nopek had worked long and hard to get out from under the debt that buying Bangor had put on his shoulders. Bangor's huge energy needs still posed a major financial burden.

Bangor, a Cudov, was one of the largest semi-intelligent creatures available to the general public. The relationship between he and Bangor was one of mutual love at first sight.

Nopek was up on the pet selection observation platform with no real intention of buying anything when Bangor approached, sniffed him, and let the warmth of her thoughts flow over him as her vertical crown scales turned an alluring yellow.

The responding intensity of the yellow light emitted from Nopek's eyes reflected the mutual attraction.

The cost of housing and feeding a Cudov never crossed Nopek's mind. If it had he might have had second thoughts.

His best bargaining powers left his time account in the red, but he rode Bangor out of the pet compound on a fully equipped head saddle.

His six hundred years of prudent saving and investing was almost erased by the purchase.

Nopek accepted that Bangor was his mid-life crisis. He worked triple time for more than three cycles to get his bank account back in the white. When his time account went farther up into the yellow Nopek scheduled their first vacation.

Nopek had forgotten how the Time Dimension Terminal with its hundreds of ten-thousand-foot-high towers supporting, thousands of interwoven purple and black two hundred parsec diameter time and dimension tunnels, aiming their transmissions across the known universe, comprised of the millions of galaxies, connecting the third and fourth world dimensions, always overwhelmed him.

It always made him feel slightly nauseated. It was no different this time.

The transmitting energy pulses distorting the light echoes reflecting back to his eyes evoked the taste of epitac in the back of his throat. The disorientation made visual light transmission and reception an energy draining challenge.

Nopek felt like a grain of issil as he sat on Bangor's head looking up at the magnetic amplification columns rising and disappearing into the fabric of space.

How it all worked, was a mystery to him. Dimensional travel had been around longer than he had existed. Nopek was a simple teller of stories about travel to the higher dimensions. This was laughable since he made most of it up as he wrote but it did put credits in his light account.

There were only two known dimensions that had actually been discovered. The fourth dimension that he lived in and the third dimension that was currently being explored.

Time dimension travelers stood at their designated vacation departure launch area and at the moment of departure there was a bright white flash followed by a pulse in the purple stream aimed at their target time and dimension destination.

The black streams with returning vacationers ended in similar bright flashes adding to Nopek's disorientation .

That sending and returning pulses were regular and steady at about the rate of Nopek's heartbeat just made things worse.

Nopek's body was inextricably tuned to the rhythm of the terminal.

The entire web of timeline streams, elevated and directed by the time towers, the flashing and pulsing of the departing and returning vacationers made the terminal a disturbing pulsing throbbing nightmare that only ended when he left the terminal.

Only the memory of the luxurious feeling of basking and absorbing the rich magnetic field of the vacation destination gave Nopek the will power to face the Time Dimension Terminal.

Nopek focused his eyes and sent his light beam toward the vacation destination screen. He let out a groan and voiced a curse when he saw the length of the departure line to his selected vacation spot. He was at the very back of a very long line.
To make matters worse there was a time snivel and its evidently inane owner immediately in front of them. The time devouring beast was restrained as required by law but only a big phanxa would own one.

Dốt nát phản xạ, Nopek cursed under his breath.

Bangor instinctively tried to protect Nopek from the snivel. Bangor was on the verge of smashing the beast.

The security guard had noticed the situation and was coming toward them with his time absorption gun out of his holster.

Nopek had to do something, or they would get sent back to the terminal entry area where they would be charged three parsacs of time and some additional reduction in light privileges.

Knowing he needed to act quickly Nopek looked for an alternative.

He needed a small miracle.

There, toward the very back of the terminal beyond the crowd of thousands, was one active terminal with no line. This was usually the sign of a less desirable location with a weak gravity field.

The lone ticket agent with his eyes dimmed stood listless in a waiting stance.

The sign behind him reflected the information that this three-dimension vacation was located in a galaxy at the far edge of the known Universe. The only scheduled vacation offering was significantly into the past, but the price was eighty percent of the ticket Nopek was holding.

The swish of the departing time travelers, the persistent taste of epitac and the size disorientation was replaced with elation and the warm feeling and the sweet taste of *oon* in Nopek's throat.

It was a no brainer. Nopek immediately directed Bangor toward the agent.

He noted Bangor's sigh of pleasure and when he looked back he could see that the owner of the snivel was retrieving it from two lines away where it had somehow ended up.

Nopek knew immediately that the *somehow* was the swish of Bangor's tail. He chuckled and tapped on one of Bangor's scales as he pretended to reprimand her.

Her response was to increase the yellow glow of her head crest in a sign of pleasure.

Their arrival brought the agent to life. He boasted about the new location that had just been opened for commercial visits and had a magnetic field second to none.

The agent pulled out the helmet that would allow Nopek to see and hear sounds on the three-dimensional world. He assured him that once he got engaged he would forget he had the helmet on.

What about my companion Nopek inquired?

It was clear from the puzzled look of the agent that he had never outfitted a Cudov. The agent put out a call and soon a transport arrived with a helmet for Bangor's head. It was good to see that the helmet design anticipated the head saddle Nopek sat on.

He had Bangor lay with her head on the floor so the three terminal personnel could put on and adjust the head gear to fit her head.

Monsters, we look like monsters Nopek thought as he took in his appearance and then looked up at Bangor. He could sense her reaction as she looked at him and her crown scaled turned a sickly greenish blue.

Any creature we meet will die when they see us Nopek commented to the agent.

The agent asked if Nopek knew that on a third-dimension world he would be invisible.

Of course, he knew, Nopek lied.

Vacationing in a three-dimensional world had never crossed Nopek's mind. He was *"considering it"* out of desperation and the fact that he would have light credits with which to buy food and pay his bills when he returned made it really attractive.

Nopek was elated when the agent immediately guided them to the launch area. He could see that the line he had been in had barely moved. Little wins like this would make up for any flatness of a three-dimensional experience.

Bangor took up almost all of the launch area. If she grew anymore they would need to make special time launch arrangements.

The feeling of falling and then being rapidly pulled up in the opposite direction once again brought the bitter taste of epitac to the back of his throat and made his insides feel like they had turned over and been kicked. The transfer was worse than he remembered from previous vacations and wondered if it was due to the fact this destination was at the farthest reach of the time dimension transport system.

He could sense Bangor diming and then her resurge as in parallel they both recovered from the transfer.

Bangor was almost immediately animated as she sensed a passing water creature almost her size with a flat tail spouting water from the top of its head and broad casting powerful blue thoughts.

Nopek was amazed and fascinated as well. What a treat and they had just arrived!

This was as unexpected as the strength of the magnetic field and the mental noise. The magnetic field was the strongest Nopek had ever experienced.

Nopek paused for a moment to take it all in and make sense of world around them.

He adjusted the viewer setting to long range.

Bangor was sitting back on her haunches in her obedient resting position. Only her head was above the fluid they had landed in.

She was such a darling.

He could sense her periodic distraction when the water creatures passed by. Some were dim and barely noticeable but there were several kinds that were loud color broadcasters. Most seemed to broadcast the more pleasant colors of light greens and yellows but there was one that broadcast in black. Nopek tried but failed to imagine its appearance.

He sent reassuring commands to keep Bangor still. Nopek was confident that Bangor was not in any danger. The black broadcasts came from creatures a third of Bangor's size and Nopek knew of no creature that could put a scratch on Bangor.

The travel agent must never have vacationed in this three-dimensional world otherwise he would have been much more excited about the intensity of the magnetic field.

It was at least twice as strong as any of the four available four-dimensional worlds the line of vacationers had chosen. Most would have loved to bask in the intensity of this magnetic field at a fraction of the cost.

The mental noise onslaught was totally unexpected, disorienting and a bit overwhelming in its intensity.

The odor of the air was ten times worse than the droppings of a Cudov and after spending three cycles shoveling up after Bangor when they were out on their morning walks, Nopek knew the worst smell possible.

Nopek rummaged through the storage locker located behind him and found the nose plugs he needed and then crawled out and put two fiber air freshening filters in Bangor's nostrils.

Her head crest turned a bright yellow in response.

It was during this lull that an intriguing mental image of a biped creature formed in Nopek's mind. But more amazing than the image was that there seemed to be an strange, melodic, golden sound that caused him to think of oon and see yellow.

He could tell it was also pleasing to Bangor because her head crest scales began pulsing, a golden yellow hue, to the flow of the sound.

Nopek realized that in the fourth dimension, sound was accompanied by accenting light and color. Here in the three-dimensional world sound seemed to be accompanied by connection to emotion and taste.

Fascinating!

Nopek began to slowly turn his head to see if the reception of his three-dimension helmet would orient the direction he needed to travel to find the source of this rapturous sound of deep emotion and such a sweet a taste.

In the distance, just to their right where the fluid met the solid, Nopek could just barely see movement.

Nopek kept Bangor moving toward the area in a slow steady pace. Their movement and the interaction of the fluid caused it to rise and wash onto the solid in repeating cycles. It would not do to have Bangor push too much fluid ahead of her.

Back against the backdrop of a jagged vertical hard grey solid wall, three areas glowed and flickered yellow and red. Nopek recalled his studies of the ancients of his world and marveled at the parallel of what he was seeing. These were beings similar to his ancestors.

The broadcast emotion and taste shifted down to one that made him want to shield his mind and dim his eyes. He felt Bangor slow and almost stop.

He and Bangor slowly moved to the boundary and onto the loose solid very similar to the grains of issil in his world. Bangor carefully lowered herself onto the issil with her snout pointed parallel to the fluid boundary. Nopek was now down to a level that allowed him to see the entire scene clearly.

He was looking at a group of bipeds very similar in structure to himself that were gathered around each of the flickering circles. The biped image that had been in his mind now physically presented itself in slight variations among a group of some forty individuals.

All had black hair down to the point where their bodies connected to two appendages with hands at their ends. Their bodies were almost a duplicate of his. The only significant differences Nopek could make out was that they had hair the color of the beams of returning vacationers, and their noses rivaled Bangor's in size.

Among his kind, hair had disappeared thousands of cycles ago and his nose was flatter and half the size of these bipeds.

The most striking contrast was that their eyes did not project any light.

Nopek imagined that they would be helpless in the dark.

In front of the group out closer to the fluid boundary was a large gathering of the same material that Nopek had observe the bipeds periodically putting into the flickering piles where they were gathered.

Nopek relaxed and leaned against Bangor's now pinkish yellow head crest. It was clear she sensed no danger and was enjoying watching these bipeds as much as he.

A change in the mental tempo, the variation in the sounds and the declaration of his presence made Nopek focus on one specific individual as it walked toward him.

This being stopped a full Bangor bodies length away and identified Nopek to be a being from beyond, from another time, another place. It implored Nopek to accept the spirit of a being referred to as Long Arrow.

Nopek knew there was nothing he could do. He had never had such an experience and the travel agent had not given him any instructions about encounters with other intelligences even though all the vacation advertisements made reference to alien encounters in a bid to make everyone think their upcoming vacation would be special. As far as he knew this would be the first contact with a being from another dimension.

Could they see him? Nopek took off his helmet and looked to see if he were visible. No, both he and Bangor were invisible just like the agent had said they would be.

Then the source of the sound, that had taken Nopek from tasting the wonders of oon to almost extinguishing the light in his eyes, strode forward with a new assault on his senses.

Smaller in physical size and to Nopek's three-dimensional vision the fairer of the two, it opened its mouth and the sound, the emotion, the taste of oon now laced with idg made Nopek want to kneel and beg her to never stop.

Nopek almost fell off of Bangor when the figure knelt to match his stance and move into yet another variation of taste and color.

Bangor's crest scales were now red trimmed in yellow and she was emitting soothing thoughts normally reserved for the Cudov young. It was clear this interaction was impacting them both.

The sound ended and the two figures turned and strode slowly back toward the rest of the gathering.

Nopek wanted to call out and beg for more.

The light provided by the star for this planet was now dimming.

Nopek' and Bangor's viewers both automatically optimized their vision based on the light level.

Nopek fine-tuned their vision to compensate for the flickering light coming from the three rings.

Once again the sound caused Nopek to taste oon at double strength as a slow procession of all the beings came walking slowly down a sloping path about as wide as the beings were tall. Each carried an item at their mid-level supported by their up turned hands. Six beings carried a flat object with a tightly wrapped seventh figure on it.

Stay, Nopek commanded Bangor as he descended from her forehead and walked closer to the place where the six were now putting the seventh figure.

Nopek walked to the fluid side of the gathering and stood watching as the body was lifted by the six and placed on top of the pile of fibrous material. Then as each person approached and put their object on the wrapped body, the sound rose to a pitch that tasted worse than epitac then came back to oon tinged with idg.

Nopek fell to his knees overcome by it all. The emotional high followed by the low was almost too much for him to take.

Bangor's reaction was to broad cast strong waves of soothing thoughts. This cycle of the worst of taste to the best of taste continued as each person placed their item and quietly broadcast sounds and thoughts that Nopek could not understand but whose color was mostly grey.

He found himself in a keeling position with his eyes transfixed on the body and his feeling cycling to the lowest of low and then to the highest of high. In his nine hundred cycles Nopek had never experienced anything like this.

Suddenly the area turned a bright white, and he could sense Bangor's towering presence and her emotional silver-grey transmission of overwhelming grief. She had come to the realization that the figure on the pyre was dead.

Nopek tore off his three-dimensional helmet in time to see what Bangor was doing.

The bright light and the wave of anguish broadcast by Bangor made all the figures around the pyre step back just in time as Bangor surgically took everything into her cavernous mouth.

Nopek alternated between watching Bangor with his helmet off and watching the same scene with his helmet on.

In three-dimension Nopek saw a brief flash of white light, felt a wave of anguish, and watched as the dead being and pyre disappeared.

Then he saw the fluid part and rays of the large bright satellite illuminate the now almost black fluid as it parted and closed, and a wave flowed away on each side.

In four dimensions Nopek watched as Bangor disappeared into the depth out to where he knew she would place the pyre in the manner of her kind.

Nopek sat down looking out to where Bangor had disappeared.

He was suddenly aware of a slender being sitting down near him and addressing him as if she could see him.

Nopek recognized her as the one with the sounds that had taken him up and then cast him down in the abyss only to be raised up again.

Her hair was pulled back and held by a black strip binding with a white beaded clasp. Her neck was encased by a string of stones. A black band went around her head across her face just above her eyes.

Her eyes even without broadcasting a light were her best feature. Her deep black eyes seemed to penetrate what Nopek knew was his invisibility

Nopek sat there spell bound as he listened to the sounds she made but also to the wave of thoughts that she broadcast.

He hoped she would let him taste oon and idg at least one more time.

In the distance Nopek could see Bangor returning.

Sitting next to him broadcasting thoughts of respect and inquire sat the maker of sounds of inspiration, ecstasy, and sadness.

Who would have dreamt that he would be was sitting on three dimensional grains of issil next to an alien Princess while high above in the pure black, surrounded by the millions of stars in this galaxy was a large white sphere.

Then as if the figure knew Bangor had returned, it stood erect and turned to the figures standing back near the three flickering circles and once again Nopek tasted oon.

This time the figures responded and threw in the idg. The back and forth of oon and idg ended with the figure stretching the oon and sweetening it beyond anything Nopek had ever experienced.

Bangor's crest scales were pulsing deep yellow to bright red.

This was their first period of a seven-period vacation. Nopek could not imagine any experience that would top the one both he and Bangor had just tasted and absorbed.

He watched as the three-dimensional beings left the issil area.

Nopek would seek them out when the three-dimension light returned.

Nopek had "settled" for what he thought would be a third-rate vacation. What he had so far experienced was beyond anything he could have imagined.

He knew at that moment that he would be a three-dimension vacation junky if he could return to this third dimensional planet, circling a third-rate star, in a third-rate solar system for a third of the price of other vacation destinations.

Bangor's slow yellow pulsing of her crest scale let him know she too was enjoying it so far and they had six more cycles to go.

The End

<u>Call me Sometime</u>

There wasn't anything he could have done about it. It wasn't his fault. He kept repeating this to himself.

He had to believe it.

He saw them being taken and he immediately ran and jumped behind the rocks. The bright beam shot past him and picked up a boulder about his size.

Buddy and Hector were pulled up into the air along with the boulder that was supposed to be him. All three winked out and were gone.

There had been no warning.

The three had been hiking along the ridge trail on a camping trip. It was getting dusk, and they were looking for a good place to camp. He had suggested the place where he was now crouching.

Buddy and Hector wanted to go up the trail and get closer to the top of the ridge. He was a little mad at his two buddies and was hanging back when the beams blinked on and came towards them.

His reaction was an immediate run for cover.

Buddy and Hector just stood looking up at the beams as if they were fireworks. They were really slow on judgment.

He figured they would be back to get him. He knew the beams shot in a straight line and you could hide from it. But he was at a disadvantage and the aliens had his friends.

He had to figure out a way to get his friends back.

What could he do?

He tried the cell phone and to his surprise the phone began to ring.

Hector answered.

Or at least he said he was Hector.

"Where are you guys and are you alright," He asked?

"I don't know where we are but were OK at the moment. We are in some kind of padded room. It's sort of like a cage. The door has a beam locking it, but you can see through. I can see down a long hallway. I haven't seen anyone yet." Hector replied.

"Well, I have got to move. I figure they will let you talk to me so they can find where I am. Call me if you learn anything that will help to get you back.

Jasper moved quickly along the trail. He was heading up but going around the back of the peak.

He was trying to figure out if the beams had come from the sky or from some object up on the ridge. He hoped it was up on the ridge. Then he would have a chance to get his buddies back.

He wanted to hide for the next hour or so and figure a plan of attack.

"I'm having delusions of grandeur," he chuckled to himself. "I'm going to outsmart and outmaneuver aliens who have "beam me up Scotty" technology," he thought to himself.

"They are using my phone to locate me. So why don't I turn it on, leave it in a specific spot and see who shows up? Let's see what the enemy looks like," he thought to himself.

He thought for a moment and then recorded a message and sent it to himself. He hoped they would analyze the phone once they had it in their possession.

He put the phone down on top of a flat rock. He wanted to make sure they would find it. The message was part of his escape plan. They might be smarter, but he wondered if they had played as many battle and espionage games as he had.

He hoped they would not be too big or fierce physically. The aliens in the games were blood thirsty and mean. He had never agreed with such a representation for beings smart enough to travel the universe.

He was hoping for smart and small.

He would see if there was a ship or some sort of object up on the ridge.

He was now moving with all the skill his Dad had taught him. He was working on becoming an Eagle Scout. He was just thirteen and a little small for his age, but he was great in the woods. He knew he was in great physical shape. He didn't boast about it, but he did two hundred sit-ups a day and sported a real six pack.

He knew how to become invisible to the eye. His friends often called him "Jasper the ghost." He was wearing his camouflage khakis. He just wasn't sure about the technology the aliens might have. He counted on them being able to do thermal scanning. It appeared that the rocks would protect him from their weapons and beams.

He worked his way along a narrow ledge. He hoped he would not meet aliens coming toward him. Maybe they would need to wear space suits to survive in the Earth atmosphere. He hoped there was some sort of leverage he could figure out.

He cautiously looked around the boulder where the trail came up over the ridge. He watched as a small spaceship landed. It did not look as big as Hector had implied when he said he was looking down a long hallway. This must be a smaller vessel sent down to get him. They probably figured he would not let them catch him with the transport beam.

"They must be planning to capture me in a more direct manner," Jasper thought.

He stayed behind the rocks and only periodically looked through a crack in the rocks to see what was going on.

He move downhill a short way and work back around above the ship. He found another rocky depression and furtively looked down on the scene from above.

He was not sure how long it had been, but it seemed to him about an hour passed. It was now getting dark. Lights came on around the vessel and two figures came out of a door in the side.

They were small.

In their suits they were about his size.

Jasper figured they were about two thirds as big as he was. He watched as the second figure did something on the side of the vessel and the door closed.

They were bipeds and had legs and arms similar to a human.

The two figures moved down the trail toward the point where he had originally disappeared.

"Not too smart," Jasper thought. "Do they think I am going to wait for them to find me?"

He got up and went down to the vessel. He hoped these were the only two.

He picked up a stone about the size of a small potato and threw it at the vessel. It landed at its base.

"No protection force field," he thought.

Jasper ran up to the vessel and opened the panel on the side. Inside was a simple lever. He pulled it and the door opened. He hoped they breathed oxygen. He did not want to suffocate.

He looked in and there on the inside was a lever similar to the one on the outside. He stepped in and pulled it down. The outer door closed.

He was in a chamber like he had seen in the Natural Geographic Deep Sea documentary.

He opened the inside door.

He tested the air. It seemed to have enough oxygen for him to breath.

It felt like the air at the top of Mount Olympus. It was thin but had enough oxygen for him to survive.

He quickly went around the vessel. He was alone. The two out searching for him were the only ones on board.

He looked for a place where he could hide.

He also looked for any monitoring cameras.

He was not sure what to look for.

He scanned what he thought was the control panel. He knew there were no windows but from the inside, the panels gave the impression of having windows on all four sides.

He was able to see three hundred and sixty degrees around the vessel. It felt like he was standing outside. He wished he could have this display to play some of his video games.

He looked around inside to see if there was a place he could hide. There was a suit storage area with two additional suits. He figured the ship was made for at least four of the Aliens. He checked out the suits and figured he would just fit in one if he needed to.

There was an area behind the back suit where he fit, and he would be totally hidden. He put his backpack in the corner and then went back to what he was calling the control room.

It was now dark outside. He wished he had his phone so he could call Hector but that was what the two figures outside were tracking.

He watched as the two came back.

They were carrying his phone and seemed to be talking to each other.

He hoped the vessel was not weight sensitive. He went back to the hiding spot and moved the last suit, so he was totally hidden.

He took several deep breaths so he could calm down. He felt his heart racing.

The two figures came in and removed their suits. Jasper wanted to look but he knew it would mean exposing his hiding spot. He did not want to take the chance.

He badly wanted to see the aliens and get an idea of their physique.

He knew the trick was to remain patient and quiet. He reduced his breathing to a slow quiet pace. He went into what he called his silent invisible mode. He had played this game with Buddy and Hector many times. They were never able to find him. He hoped it would work with the aliens.

He listened intently. He was hoping they had a spoken language. If they were telepathic he was not sure he would know how to act. If they spoke it would probably mean they had hearing as well.

This was important for him to know. He needed to understand the alien capability on a personal level. He was sure they would be technically more advanced but so far they were not very sharp about hunting and capturing.

"Book smart and woods foolish," was his Dad's saying. "I want you to be smart about both."

He hoped the vessel would return to the main ship. He figured that was where he would find Buddy and Hector. Jasper felt his stomach react to the acceleration. It was similar to a fast elevator ride.

Then there was a pop and total silence. He looked cautiously around the suit.

The light in the vessel was still on. He decided to remain in the corner. He closed his eyes and caught a few winks. He was in what he called his hibernate mode.

Not quite asleep but not totally awake. He had played this game as well.

His Dad had taught him how to remain totally still for hours and relax by going into a sort of trance. This kept him from losing track of his surroundings.

It was about an hour later when there was a bump and then everything was still.

They must have landed in or on the mother ship. He heard the hatch open and then heard it close.

He waited a few moments. He heard nothing. He went back to the control room.

The panels were still on. He could see the two figures as they walked toward what appeared to be a doorway. Two other figures were coming out toward them.

The two from the scout ship had his phone in their hands. The four looked at the phone and walked away deep in discussion.

They looked almost human. They were thin and seemed to have light fuzz on their bodies. Their eyes were located similar to human eyes, but they seemed to lack the human nose.

Jasper could not figure out where their ears were located but he knew they spoke verbally, and their mouth was below their eyes.

He watched closely as the four approached the door. It seemed to open automatically but he could not see the door move. It was more like it became permeable and they walked through it.

Jasper thought about this, and it seemed to make sense. The doors did not open, they just let stuff through. It was probably a way for the system to maintain containment integrity.

He waited another thirty minutes before trying to get to the door. While he waited he looked around to see if he could figure out how the ship worked.

He would either need to learn to fly this vessel or he would need to figure out how to get them to fly it back down with the three of them on board.

He was determined to rescue his buddies and to get them all safely back to Earth. He didn't touch any of the buttons. He was afraid the system might be self-monitoring and trigger an alarm.

To what purpose would the aliens be collecting humans?

Why arrive un-announced?

Were they afraid of upsetting the world order or afraid of the human reaction?

If they were picking up any of the shows and entertainment channels they were probably just plain scared of the crazy Human race.

They were probably an advance scouting party.

The controls seemed intuitive. There was a joystick for direction control. There seemed to be a location selection guide. The only problem at the moment was that he could not read the map that was associated with it.

After a little study he realized he was looking at a three-dimensional map of the solar system.

If he was correct the ship he was on, was on the far side of Neptune. The Earth was on the other side of the Sun.

The short ride he had been on had taken him across almost the entire solar system. The control system seemed to be a point and click design; point to where you want to go, then click go.

He would have to figure out which of the symbols meant go.

"Serious speed," he thought to himself. He wondered what technology allowed for this type of across the solar system transport in a manner of minutes.

"Really advanced race," he thought, "I wonder if they can go faster than the speed of light." Maybe they have learned to bend the fabric of space and cross over at the touch points. I would love to spend time talking these points with them."

He would risk hi-jacking the spaceship if necessary, but his first choice was to figure out how to get the aliens to return back to Earth. He was hoping they would go back once more to look for him. If they activated his phone and understood his message they would indeed return.

"Well let's see if I can find where they keep their specimen collection," Jasper thought to himself.

The only thing he took from his backpack was his multipurpose Swiss knife. He also took his small note pad and pencil. He put all of these in his big side cargo pockets.

He was about to leave the control room when he spotted what reminded him of an ID card.

It was on a string.

It was designed to wear around the neck. He picked it up and put it around his neck. Maybe it would come in handy.

Jasper cautiously looked out of the door. He scanned the landing area to make sure there was no one around. He also looked for any control rooms or viewing areas. It seemed everything was quiet.

He ran across the area to the door. He was looking for a way to open it. He bravely walked toward the door hoping it would let him through.

It did!

He stopped on the other side of the door to get his bearing. The hall went about thirty feet straight ahead and ended in a T. He decided the right-hand direction would be the one he would maintain. He was hoping he could stay oriented with the initial entrance area.

He had no idea how big this ship might be, and he did not want to be lost. It appeared the hallway he was in was a main one. There were side halls about every forty feet. Except where he had come in, the cross halls went both ways.

He could see what appeared to be a parallel hallway about forty feet to the left. He got the impression the ship he was on was about one hundred fifty feet wide.

He was going along the long hallway.

He had no idea about multiple levels. So far he had gone about two hundred feet. There seemed to be an end to the hallway about another hundred feet ahead.

He turned back to the hallway he had just passed when he heard Buddy and Hector talking.

They seemed to be located at the end of the hall going toward the side of the ship.

He approached the area cautiously. There were other rooms he could see into, but they were all empty. The aliens were not here to fill all the rooms with Humans.

He took out his pad and in large letters wrote.

"DON'T SAY A WORD.

Continue doing whatever you were doing and answer the question I write but don't give me away."

Then holding the pad so they could read it he stepped into the open.

Buddy almost blew it. But Hector interrupted him by giving him a push.

"Hey," Buddy reacted to the push and then said, "OH." He was not as sharp as Hector.

"What has happened so far," Jasper wrote?

"I wonder when anything is going to happen. Why did they bring us here if they were not going to do anything with us," Hector said.

"As a matter of fact, you would have thought they would at least have fed us," he continued.

"I have a plan to get us all back to Earth. Not a good plan but one that may work. We will need to get you two out of there and back on the small ship," Jasper wrote out on the pad.

"Do you still have your phone on you," he wrote

"I wonder if I can call home from this phone," Hector said holding up his phone.

"Call my phone and tell them you know they have it. Tell them this was our plan all along. We have been trying to verify their presence and now we have definite proof of their visit. Earth knew they had superior technology but were surprised they can travel from Neptune to Earth so rapidly. Tell them you two are special discovery agents sent out to verify their presence. If you come up missing it will verify the presence of an Alien visit. The fact they have missed capturing the third agent ensures Earth will know of their presence. The only solution is to return to Earth and release you." Jasper wrote.

He pushed his hand through the door, and it let it pass. He indicated to Hector to do the same. Hector tried but the door would not let Hector's hand through.

Jasper took off the card around his neck and tried again. The door would not let his hand go through. Now he knew how lucky he had been to find the card.

"Call now," Jasper wrote.

Hector made the call and talked into the phone.

He pointed out that the four sitting around the phone listening ought to know they were being monitored.

How else would he know to call?

"If they come to see you tell them that you two can get me to come out to meet you and them. They may decide that doing so would speed up my capture. I am going back to the scout ship and wait for all of you to come on board." Jasper wrote.

"If nothing happens, I will come back for you and we will try to escape on our own," he wrote on the last page of his small pad.

Jasper wished there was more he could do.

Once back on the ship he put the back the card just as he had found it. He had been sitting looking at the displays for about fifteen minutes when he saw a lone figure coming across to the ship. He quickly hid in his corner.

He heard the hatch open. Then some sort of exclamation and someone apparently talking to themselves. The hatch cycled again. After a few moments Jasper came out of his corner.

He went back to the control room. The card was gone. He knew getting back to his buddies would not be possible. He hoped Hector would be convincing.

He went to his hiding corner to get some rest.

He figured a discussion about what to do was probably going on in the Alien control center. He imagined they were like many organized species. They would need to discuss and come up with some sort of plan.

From what he could tell they were more advanced technically, but they did not think as aggressively as the human race.

They certainly must not have battle video games.

The door chamber cycling made him instantly alert.

He listened carefully and was overjoyed to hear Buddy and Hector in a mock argument. They were being loud for his benefit.

It was clear Buddy had taken the role of bad guy willing to give him up and Hector was playing the good guy by being mad at Buddy.

"You're a jerk. How could you be willing to trick Jasper?" Hector was saying.

This time Jasper chanced getting found out. He needed to see how the craft was controlled.

Once back on Earth he planned to hop the craft away from the landing area as a distraction. This would give the Aliens something to concentrate on while Buddy, Hector and he made their escape.

He saw there were three aliens on this trip.

The joystick seemed to be for local maneuvering and the long distant stuff was coded into the computer and handled automatically.

The ride back to Earth was amazingly fast and seemingly effortless.

He watched as the pilot used the joystick to easily maneuver the craft to the ground.

He realized their actions were very similar to what human would do.

Hector and Buddy were now arguing about who would lure Jasper out of the woods.

Only two of the three aliens were putting on suits. The two escorted Buddy and Hector out of the ship.

They didn't seem to be armed. They were probably counting on their beam technology.

Well, now he would find out how tough the aliens were.

First he looked around to see if the remaining alien had any weapons.

It did not look like he had any.

He was busy monitoring the four outside and scanning the area around the craft.

Buddy and Hector were both bracketed by a box on the screen. It appeared they were contained by some sort of beam. There was an empty box. This one was probably meant to capture him.

Jasper walked into the control room and very calmly told the remaining alien, "You are going to hop this craft away from this area about a mile. You will put it down. I will tie you up and leave you until your buddies return.

Afterwards, I suggest you leave the solar system.

Tell your leaders to come visit when they are ready to openly engage us."

He did not expect the alien to understand him, but he gestured his expectations with his hand.

The alien started to get out of his seat, but Jasper pushed him firmly back down.

He realized how light the alien felt.

Physically he was many times stronger.

He again gestured his command.

The alien got it.

Well, he figured they would be smart.

Jasper indicated his two buddies and indicated he wanted the boxes removed.

The alien got it again.

He watched as the two aliens outside realized they were being left. They turned to come back to the craft.

Buddy and Hector immediately made for the woods. They were headed down the trail to the lake. Jasper knew exactly where he would find them.

The alien jockeyed the craft to a landing about a half a mile away.

"Send a beacon to your partners so they can find you," Jasper instructed. He watched closely as the alien vocally seemed to communicate with the other two.

Jasper pulled out the cord from his knapsack. He tied the alien's hands behind his or maybe her back. He wasn't sure. This one seemed different from the other two. He would have loved to spend more time getting to know these aliens, but their introduction had been poorly executed.

"You know, we humans would love to interact with you. You are probably right to be concerned about the human race. We will soon be out, and we will compete with you. Get ready for competition. We will not be stopped," Jasper lectured as he tied the alien into the chair.

He saw his phone on the control panel.

"Call me some time when you are in town. Maybe we can get together," he said as he picked up his phone.

He got out of the spaceship and went downhill away from the ship in the opposite direction he would ultimately go.

He was not going to give them a chance to find him.

He was going to make sure they would leave empty handed on this expedition.

The End

<u>Not Normal</u>

He noticed things. He began to notice strange things going on at School. Yeah, Yeah strange things are always going on at school. But this was different. Jason began to notice everyone was starting to be nice to each other. He really noticed it when Janet Lekowski actually smiled and said hello to him. Janet Lekowski had never been nice to him. She was the meanest B__ person walking the halls of the school. She was in eighth grade. She had just said hello to him. Something was wrong, very wrong.

At lunch he decided to test his idea that something was changing the kids at school. He took his tray and sat down in the area where all the jocks always sat. This he knew was suicide. He hoped it wouldn't hurt too much.

Larry Smythe, the meanest of the mean football jocks came toward him with his tray full of food.

Jason almost got up to run away.

"Hey dude, how's it hangin? Larry asked him as if they were buddies. Larry was in ninth grade. Jason was in seventh grade. That alone was cause for getting abused.

If it had been April Fool's day maybe Jason would have believed it was a joke. Now he knew something was very wrong.

The rest of the football team showed up and acted as if Jason sitting at their table was normal. Jason hurried to finish his lunch. He had to find Jake and John. He hoped they had not been changed.

Something or someone was changing the kids. In a way it was nice, but it was not normal.

He found his two buddies sitting at their favorite spot overlooking the tennis court. They were eating their sandwiches they had brought from home. They did this all the time. The three J's as they were called, would sit on the grass, and eat in peace. The lunchroom was too dangerous and overwhelming. Jake Singleton was slender, tall, and lanky with blue eyes. John Hazelwood was almost an opposite. He was short, a little heavier build with black hair and brown eyes. Jason knew he was sort of in between. He had brown hair, more or less blue eyes and had an average build. He hoped his physique would improve with puberty.

"How are you guys doing?" Jason asked. He watched closely to see if his buddies had been changed.

"Like always, just trying to stay out of the way and not get abused," Jake replied. "Why didn't you bring your lunch?"

"Oh, I did but I was running an experiment during lunch," Jason replied.

"Hey, John that looks like a great sandwich. Is it one of your inventions? Give me a bite?" Jason said to see if John was OK.

"You must be kidding. Get your filthy germs on my masterpiece. Besides, you already had lunch," John replied as he deliberately took a huge bite out of his sandwich.

Jason felt like hugging both of them. They were still normal.

"Have you noticed anything unusual in the last couple of days," Jason asked as he waved back to two girls on the tennis court.

That was strange. No one ever waved at them. Usually, it was as if they were invisible.

"Only that you seem to be making friends with everyone around you. Who are you waving at," John mumbled through a mouthful of food.

"Yep everything is normal with John," thought Jason.

"Look, something is going on. I want you guys to help figure out what is happening.

"Today Janet Lekowski smiled and said hello to me," Jason explained.

"Are you sure you didn't imagine it. She never even looks at us. If she does it's to tell us what losers we are and to get out of her sight," Jake said without looking up.

He thought Janet was good looking, but she was mean as a snake.

"I'm sure. I did a test at lunch. I sat at the jock's table," Jason continued.

"Wow and your still in one piece," Jake looked up to see if there were any bruises.

"It was weird. Larry Smythe treated me like one of the guys. When all the rest of the team showed up they all seemed to accept me. I ate as fast as I could and got out before one of them changed their minds. Something is going on and we need to find out what it is," Jason said as he sat down on the grass besides his two friends.

The rest of the day was just as weird as the beginning. Jason was getting paranoid by the time he got on the bus. Usually this was a miserable ride home with the three of them getting ridiculed by several of the jocks. It didn't happen. The jocks just talked to each other and left the three of them alone.

"Your right, something weird is going on," Jake said as they got off at their stop.

"Yeah, this is the first time they left us alone all year. Maybe they are all taking Ritalin," John volunteered as the three walked the rest of the way home.

"Let's get together after dinner and figure out what's going on. If we are not careful we'll get the crap beat out of us because we let our guard down," Jason suggested as he got ready to go up the walk to his house.

"How was your day," he heard his mother asked from the kitchen area.

"Weird," was all he said as he went up the stairs to put his stuff in his room.

At dinner he began to wonder if whatever was going on at school was also happening at home.

Janet came in and was nice to him. A shiver ran through him as he realized she was affected.

He hurried through dinner. He wanted to talk to Jake and John. They had to find out what was going on.

They met up in Jake's tree house. This was their favorite place. They had played in it all their lives.

Now it was their quiet spot.

They often did their homework together there.

"My sisters are just as weird as the guys on the bus," John said as he climbed in through the trap door.

He was the last of the three to arrive.

Jake was an only child, so he didn't have any reference to anyone at home changing.

"What do you think is happening," he said from his corner.

"I don't know but they got my sister," Jason said in a worried voice.

"Who are they," John asked?

"We need to figure that out. We need an observation plan. We watch and see where they go, what they eat, what they drink, who they talk to. We look for anything unusual," Jason spoke up.

Jason was the organizer of the group.

Jake was the getter. He could always got whatever they needed.

John was the crafty, sneaky one. He was the one sent out on reconnaissance whenever they had to spy things out.

"We need to gather evidence. We can't have our cell phones at school but there is no rule about having a camera. Jake do you have a small digital camera we can use," Jason asked. He knew for a fact Jake had a room full every electronic and digital device imaginable.

"Yea, sure, but if we get caught taking pictures by the jocks, they'll beat us to a pulp," Jake said.

"How about it John; can you get the pictures without getting caught," Jason asked. He already knew what John would say.

"No problemo, they will never know," John said is a simulated deep voice.

John never turned down a challenge.

So, starting tomorrow, we will keep a journal and make note of what is going on. We need to know who is talking to whom and what they are saying. We can each use our spy listening devices. Let's put fresh batteries in tonight.

Every evening for the next two weeks Jason convened their meeting in the tree house. He would write down every observation, make notes next to the pictures of the kids at school. He would write down, who they were talking to, what they were saying, how they were acting.

After a week of discussing their daily experience they came to the conclusion that whatever had happened had affected everyone.

They could not find the source.

They did not see any strangers. No aliens. No conspiracy.

"I don't get it. We're missing something," Jason said as he threw down his pencil.

"Well, if it's not them, maybe it's us. Maybe puberty makes us more likable," John spoke quietly from his corner.

"Yea, and soon Janet will be after your body," Jake laughed from his corner.

"Wait a minute. Maybe John's right.

We have been observing everyone else.

What has changed for each of us?

We need to examine ourselves. Let's begin just before that first day.

Let's write down everything we can think of and see if there is something we missed that may have happened to the three of us," Jason said as he grabbed his pencil and began making notes.

"Hey, it's late.

My mom will be mad if I don't get back and get ready for tomorrow.

Tomorrow is Friday, we will have the whole weekend to figure out what happened to us.

So, it wasn't until Saturday afternoon that they put together a plan. They compared notes and found that there didn't seem to be anything out of the ordinary that had happened to the three of them. They realized they spent wayyy too much time together.

"I don't get it. What are we looking for," Jake said as he threw his pencil at the dart board.

"There has got to be something common that happened to the three of us at about the same time," Jason said as he picked up the pencil and tossed it back to Jake.

"That could have happened any day of the year," John said as he thought about the fact that they could probably more easily list the days they had not been doing something together.

"I can't recall anything unusual since the time we had to rescue John off the water tower. We were lucky we didn't get caught," Jason said as he thought back at how lucky it was they were able to blindfold John and get him to come back down from the tower.

He had been alright until they got to the top and looked down. Then he froze.

"Yea, but what if we were mind wiped. We wouldn't remember a thing," John pointed out.

"Hey, I think you got something. We wouldn't have to be mind wiped. It could have been put in our Kool Aid or our food. Maybe it was a movie we watched, like the one where everyone dies but instead we become popular. Not so bad when you come to think about it," Jake continued the thought.

"Yea maybe, but when your sister treats you nice, it's weird. That means it's not real or normal. Gives me the shivers," Jason countered.

"OK, I agree. So how are we going to find out what's going on," Jake asked as he threw his pencil at the dart board again.

"Let's begin by putting together a list of all the people who would be able to do something like this," Jason suggested.

They worked for the next hour putting together a list of people.

"Let's rate each person as to whether we think they would do such a weird thing," John suggested.

"For instance, I think we can drop my two sisters. They liked being mean to me. For all I know they may be suffering from all of this being nice," he continued.

"Yea, I think sisters are out," Jason agreed as he scratched out his sister's name.

"I would put our Dad's low on the list. They are usually nice. When they want us to do something like trying out for soccer or field hockey they just tell us to go do it. No questions asked," Jake offered.

"Ok, we leave them on the list but put them toward the end of our investigation," Jason said moving the Dads down on the list.

"You know that puts our teachers and mothers at the top of the list," John observed.

"I don't think the teachers are going to screw with our minds other than give us too much homework," Jason said.

"Wow that leaves our mother's at the top of the list. Now I am afraid," Jake said in a hushed voice.

"Let's begin with a sweep of the club house to make sure we are not being observed or listened to. Then we need to do the same for our rooms. Even our clothes need to be examined. If the three of them are into something together we are in trouble," Jake said as he looked out of the window of the club house and then looked down the hatch.

He half expected one of the mother's to be on the steps listening.

"Your right, this is going to be tough if they are the ones. We will first need to make sure we are not under surveillance. Then we need to come up with a way to monitor what they are doing. We also need to start making our own lunch. They may be poisoning us," John said as he got into it.

"I thought you already made your own sandwich," Jason countered.

"Yea, but you guys don't and sometimes we share. I don't want your mothers poisoning me," John said as if he was the main victim.

"Let's start observing them and logging down what they are doing and who they are talking to. Today we will make sure they are not listening or observing us. I don't think so. They are just now getting use to the internet, face book and being friended.

We are the ones who are keeping track of everything and everybody. We are the ones who just aren't paying attention," Jason rambled.

Tomorrow after church we are all going out to eat. This will give us a chance to see if there is anything weird going on.

Jason went home. There he found his sister was still treating him nice. He knew something was wrong. He tried to start a fight with her by stealing a shrimp from her plate at dinner.

"Oh, do you want another," Janet pushed another of the shrimp pieces toward him.

"Uh, thanks but I have had enough," he said as shiver ran down his back. He was watching his mother. She seemed not to be paying attention. His dad was focused on eating as always.

"You and your buddies have a nice day," his Dad asked looking a little puzzled.

"He has no clue," Jason thought as he watched his Dad.

He was becoming more certain whatever was going on, his mother was behind it. She was the one who seemed to be avoiding eye contact.

After dinner, he decided to "clean" his room. He took everything off the shelves. He was dusting each of his trophies and all the other clutter on the shelves. This gave him a chance to examine every item. Once he got everything back on the shelf, he pulled his chest of drawers away from the wall and cleaned behind it.

He found his old library card. He no longer needed it because the library had upgraded to a password for checking stuff out. He took out all his clothes and put them back.

The closet was next.

Then he checked the bed.

By bedtime he had cleaned his whole room.

He took his shower sure he was not being monitored.

He went downstairs to say good night.

"What were you doing all evening," his Mother asked.

"I decided to clean my room," Jason answered truthfully.

"Really, are you feeling OK," his Dad asked looking up from his e reader.

"Remember, Church tomorrow and were going to the Brazilian barbeque afterwards," his mother said as she gave him a good night kiss.

Janet looked up from the table where she was on her computer and said goodnight.

Jason almost ran out of the room. He locked the door to his bedroom and then took the straight back chair and propped it under the doorknob. He checked to make sure his window was locked.

He couldn't remember falling asleep, but it must have happened. He looked at his alarm clock and groaned. It was five in the morning.

He looked out the window. It was still dark.

He rolled over but could not get back to sleep. He cursed under his breath. Why was this happening? He thought about the movie where everyone was taken over.. The body, snatchers he thought.

He sat on the edge of his bed. He saw the blinking light on his phone. John had sent him a text. He was awake too.

"My sisters were both nice to me last night,"

"Yeah, mine too,"

"I didn't get much sleep last night,"

"I was OK once I cleaned my room and propped the chair under the door handle"

"I wish I would have thought of that. I kept waking up all night,"

"Yeah, and I slept in this morning. I wonder how Jake did?"

"Well, he doesn't have sisters being nice and scaring the living day light out of him,"

"See you in church,"

"CU"

It was six when he went down to the kitchen for a bowl of cereal.

"Heavens, what are you doing up so early," his mother asked when she came down around seven.

"Oh, I woke up early this morning. I decided a bowl of cereal would hit the spot," Jason said as he thought about asking his mother what was going on.

He decided to wait until later that day or maybe the next.

He was afraid of what she might tell him.

"Well aliens have arrived, and they are going to take over the world and I am helping. Or maybe, "The other world has taken over my soul and I have given them possession of my son," these were just a couple of lines that ran through his mind as he watched her making pancakes.

He hoped the pancakes were ok to eat. They smelled delicious. He loved to have two pancakes submerged in syrup with two over easy eggs on top with a sausage on the side. He had gotten that vice from his father. You would have expected his Dad to be overweight the way he ate but he was still skinny.

"Well, you are up early," his Dad said as he walked around the stove to give his wife a kiss.

"My Dad doesn't have a clue," Jason thought as he watched the two.

He was definitely off the suspect list. He needed to be put on the clueless list.

The pancakes and eggs were as good as always. They had this treat about once a month.

He would probably fall asleep in church. He sure hoped so. Once in a while one of the Priests would come up with a good sermon but usually he was bored stiff.

After breakfast he went upstairs and got ready for church. He didn't see Janet until it was time to get in the car and drive to church. John and he went to the same church. Jake and his family seldom went to church at all.

John's Mom and his Mother sat together. John and he sat almost directly behind them. The sisters sat to John's right. Jason liked to sit in the very first place in the pew. That way he had a place to rest his head when he wanted to dose off.

As he walked up to take communion, he wondered if the wine had been doctored. He hadn't thought of that before. He was becoming paranoid. They had to solve this problem soon or he would go nuts. He looked at the other people in the church to see if there was anything strange with them.

After Church, the sisters decided they wanted to ride together to the Brazilian Churrascaria restaurant. He and John got into the back of the car.

"How have the two of you been doing," John's Mom asked looking back at them over her shoulder.

"OK" was the single word response both John and he gave in unison. That was the extent of the conversation all the way to the restaurant.

Jake and his Mom and Dad were already at the restaurant when they got there. They had already gone to their table. Jake had saved them two chairs with their backs to the wall.

To Jason the situation was awkward. The three of them went and got some of the makings around the salad bar. Jason liked the palm hearts, with olive oil and some salt. He also liked the large olives. He took one piece of Sushi just to try it.

The sisters were still being nice which seemed really strange. Their mother's kept looking at each other and then at the three of them. It was all pretty weird.

Jason concentrated on selecting the cuts of meat he liked best. The meat just kept coming until he turned his disk over to show the red "Stop" signal. John just kept right on eating. He was the smallest of the three, but he could eat more than any one of them.

"Hey, you girls are sure eating a lot. You'll get fat," John tried to agitate his sisters.

"You're so right. We should stop eating so much," his oldest sister said as she turned her card over to red and the other two girls followed her.

"Pass me the bottle of crazy sauce," Jason thought as he watched the scene unfold! A normal response would have been, "Mind your own business, you pig!"

Later back in the club house Jason recounted the incident.

"Yeah, that almost cracked me out. I had to bite my tongue to keep from saying anything," John volunteered.

"Did it seem like our mothers were watching us," Jake spoke up. He had been quiet the whole time they were together. "I think they have done something and are trying to decide if everything is OK. I think the three of them are our culprits. I just don't have any idea what it is they have done and that scares me," Jake said as he threw a dart at the board.

Jason decided to move. It was one thing when Jake threw pencils at the board, but it was serious when he started to throw darts.

"So, what are we going to do about this? How are we going to find out what is going on?" Jason pondered.

"Why don't we just ask them what they have done," John suggested.

"Really, do you think they'll just tell us," Jason pondered?

"Not my mother, or your mother but Jake's mother would tell Jake," John pointed out.

"I think your right. Jake how about if you ask your mother why everyone is treating us so different," Jason said looking expectantly at Jake.

Jake threw all three darts at the board.

He was really good. He had thrown these darts thousands of times.

All three darts hit the bull's eye.

He left the darts on the board.

"OK, I'll ask but I am bothered by what it all means if they are doing something to us," Jake pondered.

"Yeah, I'm scared about this too, but we have to find out what's going on," Jason said as he pulled the darts off the board.

He only threw darts when he was nervous, and Jake and John always moved to his side of the club house when he was throwing darts.

"How are you going to ask," John spoke up.

"I'll ask tonight. I will wait until after dinner.

Mom and I normally eat dessert and Dad goes into the family room and watches the news.

I'll just blurt it out. I don't know how else to do it," Jake replied.

"Why don't you first tell her, everything is OK and the three of us know something is not normal. Let her know we are just trying to find out what's going on. Ask her if she could help," John said quietly.

"Whoa, dude. When did you become such a smooth talker," Jason said looking at John with new appreciation for his friend.

"Well, its dinner time. I'll text you guys if I find something out. Otherwise, I'll see you in the morning for the bus ride to school," Jake said as he went down the steps from the club house.

There was no text message. John and Jason were standing together waiting for the bus. They let out a collective sigh of relief when they saw Jake walking toward them, but they could tell by his walk that something was bothering him.

"My mother said she would tell me, but I would have to wait until tonight. We were right. It is our mothers. Tonight, after dinner, we are all getting together at my house; our parents and the three of us. The sisters are out. My mom said she would arrange it." Jake shared as they sat at the back of the bus.

Janet Lekowski was still being nice.

The jocks left them alone.

They sat together overlooking the tennis court and the girls waved at them.

They were in an alien world, and they were in a daze.

The normal conversation was missing.

They weren't arguing, they weren't complaining about the homework, they were thinking about what they would find out that evening.

The bus ride did not come too soon.

The walk up to his house seemed a mile long to Jason.

A shiver ran through him as he opened his front door.

"How was your day," his mother called from the kitchen.

"How was my day? You ask how my day was. What did you expect my day to be," ran through his mind?

"OK," he called back and walked up the stairs to his room and closed the door. He took the chair and put it under the doorknob.

He heard his Dad come home and Janet was talking about a party she had been invited to. Jason figured it was safe for him to go downstairs.

For once he was glad Janet wanted to talk about her party invitation and who was going to be at the party.

After Janet left the table to go do her homework, his Mom made the announcement. The three of them were to be at the Singleton's for a quick discussion this evening. The Hazelwood's would be there too.

"What this about? Have the boys gotten into some sort of trouble?" Dad asked.

Jason knew his Dad was clueless about what had been going on. In a way this was comforting to him.

A little later the three of them walked down the street to the Singleton's. Jason saw John and his family approaching from their street. They walked up the walk together. Jason and John dropped to the back.

"Come on in. Let's go to the living room," Jake's mom said as if it was a Sunday get together.

The three Moms stood together in one group, the Dads had each taken a seat and Jason, Jake and John sat on the floor cross legged.

Jake's Mom began the explanation, "Dr. Winston suggested we try a new pheromone treatment that helps improve the social acceptance of kids who seem to be on the fringe of their peer group. Since the boys seemed to be getting bullied and pushed about, we thought it was a good idea.

Dr. Winston said most patients didn't even notice the change and almost all thought it was great. Many kids have gone from being out cast to being in the in group.

She said we could try it and to see if it would help. She suggested not making a big thing of it and just including it with the routine vaccination shots the school required.

So, we agreed to try it. You have to get monthly shots to maintain its affect."

"Honey, I'm sorry if it has caused you a problem," she said with tears in her eyes as she looked a Jake.

"Yes, we were just trying to give you a chance to fit in," Jason's mom said next.

"I'm sorry I didn't check with you first," John's mom said.

"Am I the only one who thinks this is totally stupid as well as wrong," Jason's Dad spoke up.

Jason, John, and Jake sat quietly as the argument among the adults got heated. They stood quietly up and walked out of the room. Back in the clubhouse the three talked it out.

"Pheromone treatment, Janet Lekowski still probably dislikes all of us, but we smell good to her. That's just gross," Jason said.

"Yea, I would rather have them acting like they think versus acting like they smell," Jake volunteered.

"It's too bad we don't have these pheromones naturally. Are the popular kids popular because of pheromones?" John said to no one in particular.

"Well, I'm for letting nature do its thing naturally. Maybe the three of us can change some of our habits and be more social. We can begin by including other folks who seem to be having trouble fitting in. But first we need to put a stop to us being guinea pigs. I will never go back to Dr. Winston again. She always did make me nervous. I am going to my Dad's doctor," Jason spoke up.

"I agree. I am going to do the same thing," John spoke up.

"Me too," Jake agreed.

For the next few weeks Jason said hello to Janet Lekowski. Finally, the day he was waiting for happened.

"Stop saying hello to me you wad. You are so gross and disgusting. Get lost," was Janet's reply to his greeting.

"No sitting at the jock's table today," he thought with a grin.

At lunch he met his two buddies on the lawn. The girls on the court waved.

He waved back.

"Well, the three us will have to go check this out," Jason thought.

Being Normal was nice.

The End

<u>Book of Time and Space</u>

The words were stuck in her head. It was worse than having a musical lyric that would not leave you alone.

She kept trying to think of other things, but the words kept bringing her back. She and her friends had left school enthused about their summer.

They planned to go to a concert in Atlanta.

Then there would be a cruise with their parents to the Bahamas. The ship would have all sorts of activities away from their parents. It would be a great week.

Then there would be a couple of trips water skiing on the lake.

Perfect summer she thought.

Then she heard the words and the world around her changed. She began to see the frayed edges, the deteriorating condition of her neighborhood, her mother's creasy hair and her father's pot belly.

"What in the world is going on," Claudia thought to herself as she looked into a cracked mirror and realized the reflection of an ugly girl was her.

Claudia looked away shaking her head.

She went to see her older sister. She was surprised to find her sitting quietly on the edge of her bed. She was looking at the computer screen across the room.

"You heard the words today, didn't you," Clarissa said without looking.

"Yes, but what do they mean," Claudia replied.

"I don't know, you have been doing the translating," said Clarissa.

"But I don't know where to…

Suddenly a huge explosion rocked the house and hole was ripped through the wall.

Claudia found herself holding Clarissa in her arms.

"Run, I will be OK," Clarissa said through gritted teeth.

Claudia hesitated for a moment as she gathered her thoughts. She went quickly to her room and grabbed her empty school backpack. She threw in a few critical things from her chest of drawer, grabbed her tablet from her desk and then went down to the kitchen. The place was a mess. She grabbed the bottle of olive oil.

She was on her way to Silvia's house when the next explosion knocked her down.

She saw the Rawlin's house vaporize in front of her eyes. There as just a hole where the house had once stood. She hoped Mr. and Mrs. Rawlin were both at work.

She got up and ran as fast as she could. It was only two more blocks.

She was knocked down as she turned the corner. She was about to get angry when she realized she was looking at her best friend. Silvia's face was white, and she was shaking. The two turned to stare back to where a whole neighborhood had been vaporized. Silvia's house was part of the missing homes.

"Are your parents at work," Claudia asked quietly.

"Yes, they left about fifteen minutes before it a happened," Silvia said through tearful eyes.

"We did this didn't we" Silvia said through her tears.

"We need to keep on the move, a whole city block. They seem to be getting more desperate." Claudia said as she took Silvia's hand and began to run toward downtown.

"We need to get to the Library. We need to close the book," Claudia said looking back over her shoulders at Silvia.

"What do the words mean? You heard them too." Silvia cried her words as tears kept running down her cheek.

"I thought we had imagined it. The creature just can't be real. It had no mouth so how could it have spoken to us," Claudia replied.

She was looking around and realized that everything seemed to be more of a shadow then solid. Other things seemed to be simmering. They seemed almost alive.

The city park to their right just blinked out. It was gone. There was no explosion just, blink and it was gone. This time Claudia could see movement in the black where the park had been.

"They will soon figure out how to cross over," Claudia said quietly.

"Who are you talking about," Silvia whimpered.

Claudia increased her speed. She needed to get back to the basement of the library where it had all started.

The library stood just past where the park had once been. It was not a large library, but it was unique in that it had once been a church. The church goers had abandoned it when they built a brand-new church at the edge of town. It had remained empty for almost a hundred years. It was periodically used by various organizations for meetings, but it was always eventually abandoned.

Some fifty years ago an old man came into town with a load of books and set up the library. No one knew where the old man had come from, but he seemed harmless, and the town leaders figured a library was a good thing for the town to have. It would make the town more of a city.

And so it was.

The town of Elsmore became Elsmore City.

The book collection grew and soon the school system began to support it and provided a librarian.

No one knew where the old man went.

They could not remember his name.

However, they did put up a bronze statue of an old man on the fiftieth year of the libraries opening.

Librarians never throw a book away. So, the old books slowly made their way to the basement where they remained untouched until Clarissa, Claudia and Sylvia became curious about the books in the basement.

They had discovered the Cabinet almost by accident.

The Cabinet they were interested in was an old locked hard wood cabinet. The wood seemed thick and heavy.

How had the cabinet ever been carried down the steps to the basement?

The three measured the cabinet and decided it had been built in the basement.

They searched for the key to the lock, but no one seemed to know where the key might be.

It was Claudia who decided to pick the lock.

She took a picture of the lock through the keyhole. She imported the picture to her computer and made it as big as she could. She could actually see the notches and spaces for the key. She copied the pattern.

She then played with the scale of her drawing until she thought it was the size of the actual lock.

Then she made a pattern on a piece of paper.

The three took the pattern to the high school metal shop and got one of the older boys to make a brass key from the pattern.

They had made up a story about the key for the city, blah, blah, blah to satisfy the curiosity of the boys in the shop.

It had been fun creating the story.

The story had been prophetic.

A few days later they had returned to the basement of the library with key in hand. The key went in smoothly, but it would not turn. Claudia had come prepare.

She painted the key with some of her mother's old white out. It was hard to imagine that her mother still had an old typewriter and a bottle of still useable white out.

Claudia carefully slipped the key in, jiggled it, and gave it a firm twist. Then she pulled it out and proudly showed Clarissa and Sylvia her handy work.

"See you can see where the teeth of the keys met the edges of the groove. I went online and they had a picture just like the key," Claudia informed the two as she took out a small file she had brought from her father's collection from the garage workbench.

She proceeded to file the teeth down until the file met the white out still on the key. She carefully rounded the edges of each of the teeth. This had also been on the online instructions.

"Stand back, I will now open the cabinet," Claudia said making a grand gesture and bowing.

The key went smoothly in. Claudia could feel the teeth go smoothly into the grooves.

Then it seemed to get stuck.

"Here, let me try. I am a little stronger than you," Clarissa said as she moved Claudia's hand away from the key. She gripped the key with both hands and twisted. It at first appeared she would fail but ever so slowly the key moved and then there was a loud, "Clunk".

Sylvia pulled on one handle and Claudia pulled on the other. It took all their strength. They could hear the air rush into the cabinet as the doors slowly swung open. The door had been airtight. It was clear some sort of tar or old rubber seal had gone all the way around the door.

The cabinet went from the ceiling to the floor. It had three columns of shelves. But there was only one huge book in the middle of the middle shelf.

"Maybe we should go and get the librarian," Clarissa spoke up

"Are you kidding? We spent almost a week trying to figure out how to get in. Now we find an old book and you want to get the librarian. Get real. We are going to see what the book is about," Claudia said as she tried to lift the book out.

"Come you two, give me a hand," she demanded.

This effectively ended the idea of getting the librarian. The three grunted and groaned but finally lifted the book out and took it over to the only table in the basement. It must have been built about the time the cabinet had been made. It seemed to be of the same design.

The book looked as if it belonged on it.

"It's got a strap and it's locked," Clarissa groaned. "We're going to need to make another key."

"No look, I think that is the key," Sylvia said as she pointed to where a key lay on the left-hand shelf in the cabinet.

Claudia walked over to the cabinet and retrieved the key and walked back to the book. The key slipped in and turned effortlessly. The strap fell to the table.

The three stood looking at the book.

"What do you think it's about," Sylvia asked.

"It's the book of life," Clarissa countered.

"No, it was sealed away to keep it out of circulation. I bet it is a book of magic and spells," Claudia said in almost a whisper.

"Quit talking like that. You're scaring me," Sylvia said giving Claudia a punch in the arm.

Claudia slowly lifted the heavy leather cover of the book. The title page immediately alarmed the three of them.

"Let's close it and put it back," Clarissa said is a trembling voice.

Claudia slowly traced the tail and followed the body of the gargoyle to the luminous eyes on the snarling face on the right-hand corner. She took out her phone and took a picture. She flipped the page and saw strange symbols.

"It looks something like the symbols in the Egyptian display we saw in Atlanta," She said as she took another picture.

Together the three carried the book and put it back on the shelf. They closed and locked the door and went out into the bright sunshine of the June sunshine.

"Let's stop and get a smoothie. We can use the computer to get online at the Smoothie shop. I just sent the pictures to myself. We can see if there is a translator we can use," Claudia suggested.

"I'm all for it, that book gave me the creeps," Clarissa spoke up.

"I'm for the smoothie besides all the guys hang out there," Sylvia chimed in.

The translation came back quickly. It was Egyptian.

The title translated into, *"Book of Time and Space; Door to the other life."*

The first Chapter title translated into: *Opening the Door*

The other words were not translated but were marked and rewritten like phonics so the words could be sounded out.

"Look, we will be able to speak the words, but we will need a better translator if we are going to understand what we are saying.

"Wow, I wonder what opening the door means? It seems pretty scary; maybe even dangerous. I think we should get Mrs. Henry to get one of the University professors to come out and look at the book." Clarissa gave her sage advice.

"Well, I vote we go back tomorrow and get pictures of some of the other chapter titles and get them translated. I'll look for a better translation engine tonight. Maybe we can get one that will tell us what door we might open," Claudia responded and then took a long drag of her smoothie.

She was watching the reaction of Clarissa and Sylvia.

The better translator didn't help much. It did clarify that they were opening the door of time and space. But there was no better translation for the writing on the page.

Late the next morning the three once again carried the giant book to the table. This time they noticed each chapter page had weird figures drawn around the margins. Claudia took pictures of each chapter page. She wasn't sure what made her do it, but she took a picture of the very last page. It was the only other page with a drawing in the margin. This drawing was different than any other drawing in the book. It was clear it had been drawn after the book had been printed.

"Ok, let's put the book back," Clarissa said as she grabbed for the front cover of the book.

"Wait let me see the first chapter again," Claudia said flipping all the pages back to the right.

"Yea, here these symbols say, and she clumsily pronounced the translation she had gotten the day before. There seemed to be an immediate change in the room.

Sylvia let out a scream as a thing or person or something appeared from nowhere. It, he, whatever mumbled something. They all heard the words, but the creature had no mouth. Yet all three heard him, it. It seemed to float up the stairs and out of the room.

It seemed to have passed through Clarissa.

Claudia flipped the book shut and locked it. The three put it back on the center shelf and locked the cabinet. They ran out of the Library and all the way home.

It was a bright clear day.

By the time they got to their neighborhood all three were laughing hysterically.

They were convinced they had imagined the whole event. But the words would not leave them.

After dinner, Claudia put her pictures on her computer and copied the words into the translator. She began with the writing on the last page. The words talked about closing the doors to the other life.

What a weird book. She wished she could understand it better. She realized every chapter presented another door to open. Each used most of the same words as the first chapter but had a few different ones toward the end. It was getting late when she finished.

The computer was located in Clarissa's room.

Clarissa complained about not feeling well.

"You don't look so good either," Claudia said as she realized Clarissa was really looking awful.

She was a pasty white.

Clarissa was the pretty one in the family.

Claudia had freckles and was sort of a tomboy.

Sylvia was the one that attracted all the attention from the boys.

Claudia looked in the mirror and realized she wasn't looking too good either. She decided it was time for bed.

Claudia suddenly realized she was running at full speed toward the library. She realized she had been thinking back over the events of the last few days.

"Don't leave me," Sylvia shouted from behind.

"Come on we have to hurry. There isn't much time left," Claudia shouted back.

They reached the door to the library and found it locked.

"Of course, it's locked. It's Sunday," Claudia groaned within.

She looked around and then remembered the basement windows. She wondered whether the one at the end of the room was still open. She ran around to the rear of the church.

"YES, it was still open. Thank you, Thank you, Thank you," She said out loud.

"Come on help me open the window all the way, then we can climb in," She said to Sylvia.

"You seem to be getting fainter, How do I look?" Claudia asked as she looked at Sylvia.

"You don't look like yourself, but all your freckles are gone," Sylvia replied.

"We have to hurry," was all Claudia said. She was feeling really weird, feeling sort of hollow.

The window wasn't too hard to open. It fell inward on its hinges. They would have to be careful not to break the glass when they climbed in. Claudia went in first.

She dropped to the floor and looked around. An old straight back chair was in the corner. She brought it over to the window. She stood up on it.

"Pass me my backpack. Then come in backwards and on your stomach," she instructed Sylvia.

"You seem to be getting lighter. I think we are slowly vaporizing. Let's hurry," Claudia said as she realized Sylvia weighed almost nothing.

The two went immediately to the cabinet and got the book. It was all the two could do to get it to the table. It seemed to take forever to flip to the back of the book.

"BOOM" It seemed half of the room disappeared. "BOOM" Claudia could see across the park to the houses on the other side. More of the strange creatures were moving toward them.

Sylvia was screaming at the top of her voice, "Close the DOOR. CLOSE THE DOOR."

Claudia put her finger to the words on the last page and slowly and deliberately pronounced the words.

BOOM, BOOM.

She could hear the words as she recited them.

The room reappeared.

There seemed to be a strange and continuous trembling.

The strange figure came back down the stairs to the basement and merged back into the book.

The words opening time and space disappeared from her mind.

Sylvia seemed to be going back to being beautiful again.

"Let's lock the book back into the cabinet," Claudia said as she grabbed the olive oil from her bag. She applied the oil all the way around the seal. She wanted the cabinet to be perfectly sealed again.

Later she would have to figure out how to hide the book better.

Claudia and Sylvia were just coming up the stairs when Clarissa knocked on the library door.

"Are you two OK," she called out.

She had come running over as soon as the damage to her room disappeared.

Sylvia opened the front door.

The park was back. The three of them hugged each other.

"You did it. You saved the world." Clarissa said.

The three walked away hand in hand.

They did not see an old man with the brass key in his jacket pocket, the huge book clasped to his chest disappear around the corner of the Library.

By the time they got home they were talking about what they would do on the cruise to the Bahamas.

The End

Ron Mueller

<u>About the Author</u>

Ronald E. Mueller
remwriter95@gmail.com

Ron grew up in what is now Flint River State Park in Southeast Iowa. The 170-year-old house Ron lived in is built into a hillside. It faces a 125-foot-high cliff towering over the little Flint River. The house and the land talked to him about; the passing of time, the struggle to conquer the land, the struggles people faced and the wonder of nature.

He climbed the cliffs, crawled into the caves, dove from the swimming rock, collected clams from the bottom of the pond, gigged and skinned frogs for their legs. He trapped muskrats for fur, hunted raccoon in the dead of night, and with only a stick hunted rabbits in the dead of winter.

His young life was outdoors, and nature tested him.

He walked to a one room stone schoolhouse uphill both ways. A stern but warm-hearted teacher, Mrs. Henry was instrumental in shaping his character as she shepherded him from the fourth to the eighth grade. A Montessori before its time. It was a great way to grow up.

His experiences inter-twined with snippets of fantasy lend themselves to the adventures he leads the reader through.

His US Navy Service, his experiences off the coast of Vietnam, his qualification to be a nuclear reactor operator and the time in Idaho, his thirty trips around the world and visits to some sixty-five countries are all experiences that he now draws on as he writes his stories.

Ron Mueller

Short Story Collection

Ron Mueller

Published by: Around the World Publishing LLC.

QR Links to
ATWP.US web site